# Some Impropriety Expected

AMY LAURENS

# OTHER WORKS

SANCTUARY SERIES

Where Shadows Rise
Through Roads Between
When Worlds Collide

KADITEOS SERIES

How Not To Acquire A Castle

STORM FOXES SERIES

A Fox of Storms And Starlight

SHORTER WORKS AND COLLECTIONS

April Showers
Bones Of The Sea
Darkness And Good
Dreaming Of Forests
It All Changes Now
Of Sea Foam And Blood
Rush Job
The Ice Cream Crown Skating Races
Trust Issues

NON-FICTION

How To Plan A Pinterest-Worthy Party Without Dying
How To Write Dogs
How To Theme
How To Create Cultures
How To Create Life
How To Map
The 32 Worst Mistakes People Make About Dogs

Find other works by the author at www.amylaurens.com

# Some Impropriety Expected

INKLET #88

AMY LAURENS

www.inkprintpress.com

Print ISBN: 978-1-922434-28-9
eBook ISBN: 9798201787806

www.inkprintpress.com

*National Library of Australia Cataloguing-in-Publication Data*
Laurens, Amy 1985 –
Some Impropriety Expected
42 p.
ISBN: 978-1-922434-28-9
Inkprint Press, Canberra, Australia
1. Fiction—Fantasy—Epic  2. Fiction—Short Stories

First Print Edition: August 2022
Cover photo © Pexels via Pixabay
Cover design © Inkprint Press
Interior art © Amy Laurens

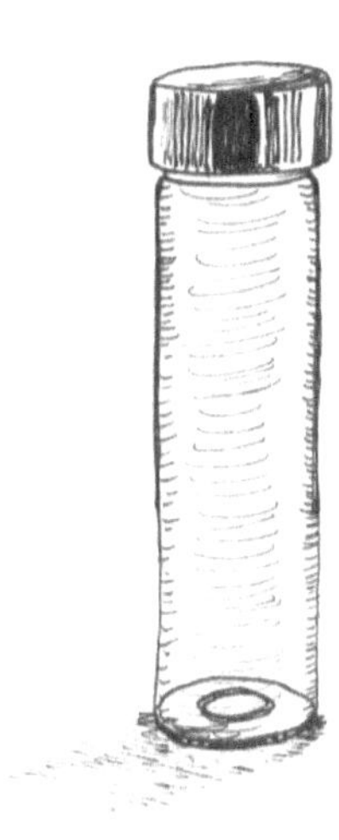

# SOME IMPROPRIETY EXPECTED

Nobody suspected Skribs of being an assassin, and that was his strength. At six-foot-three with limbs that had never outgrown their gangliness and a smile too big for his face, people tended to assume he was still a harmless, good-natured kid.

To be fair, he was.

Except for the kid part.

Lorelei had been an assassin too, at least until her ascension to the throne five years ago. Five-foot-three, with blonde hair down to her hips in its braid and hands so tiny she had to wear child-sized gloves, people tended to assume that she was still a fragile, slightly-serious princess.

To be fair, she did tend to be serious.

Only now, she was a slightly-serious queen.

She'd never been fragile.

Skribs knew that, and loved it best about her; childhood friends, they'd vowed to have either other's backs forever and all time—and just because she was now the queen, that hadn't changed a jot.

And so, as the courtiers in their metallic-thread finery, feathers in their puffy hats and crystals in their hair, pearls upon their fingers and ironstars round their necks, all stiffened in shock in the palace's receiving hall, Skribs came immediately to attention.

He barely noticed the severed head that tumbled to the ground from the wooden box, delivered by an ambassador from the North. It was a Northern ambassador: some impropriety was to be expected.

To be sure, Skribs noted the blood splatter upon the travertine floor that indicated the death was recent; mentally changed his map of the room to avoid that section in case the footing was precarious; added the ambassador to the list of people he'd sooner see dead than alive.

But he was busier staring at another man, across the far side of the hall, who alone seemed less horrified by the severed head than satisfied at Her Majesty's reaction to it.

Though—Skribs cast her a glance—Lorelei hadn't in fact reacted to it at all. Not yet. She stood stock still yet, only the slight shift in light from the silver buttons and strips of braid across her formal coat showing that she breathed at all.

Skribs pursed his lips.

He knew what followed a look like that, that moment of perfect stillness, and it was death.

But the man across the way was still staring at Lorelei, keenly, too keenly, and Skribs' senses were on alert.

Slowly, he began moving his way around the room, drifting with apparently aimlessness while the courtiers recovered themselves and began to murmur about the head, the young head, the head of Lorelei's cousin who had not yet turned one-and-twenty.

The smell of blood was in the air, and it spoke some measure of Skribs' life thus far that the way it mingled strangely with the taste of wine in the back of his throat was actually somewhat familiar.

The other man was moving now as well, drifting just as Skribs was, circling slowly closer to Lorelei, his eyes still sharp, still keen, his narrow face pinched like a hawk.

Skribs smoothed down the flap of his coat pocket.

The familiar lump of his favourite glass vial greeted his fingers.

Perfume drifted past, the smell of white rose and lily. It was a favourite amongst some of the courtly ladies right now, but he hated it; reminded him too much of his mother's funeral, where his sister had insisted on such a gaudy display of flowers that white lilies still interrupted his dreams with teeth and long, twisting tongues. Skribs wrinkled his nose, kept moving.

The man was close, now, to Lorelei, staring hungrily as she motioned for her sword.

For a moment, Skribs' heart tripped in his chest. This wasn't the Lorelei he knew, to draw sword in front of everyone and strike the ambassador down.

Did she mean for a war?

They wouldn't win, not if it began like that, and…

Skribs, despite his training, couldn't help himself: like every single person in the room, he inhaled sharply as Lorelei lifted the sword to the side of her head, and with one clean swipe cut the long rope of her hip-length braid.

She held the blonde hair aloft, a hint of fury surfacing in her dark eyes.

Skribs' heart remembered how to beat; he exploited the moment to draw close to the hawk-faced man, who even now was reaching under his coat as though he meant to draw a weapon.

So. Lorelei *did* mean to start a war, did she? For that was what the severed braid signalled, and the ambassador clearly knew it—and just as clearly had not expected it. Not like that.

Skribs clamped his hand firmly around the wrist of the hawk-faced man just as the man drew a wicked knife from its sheath, and watched as only a few paces away, the ambassador's face paled in response to Lorelei's declaration of war.

Lorelei leaned in close to the ambassador, somehow seeming to loom over a man who had half a foot on her in height.

Skribs smiled grimly. Good for her.

He knew she'd be disappointed.

Knew she'd wanted to do this the bloodless way—that was what the last five years had been all about, trying to prove that the old ways, the ways of blood, weren't needed any more. But woe betide those kings who had crossed her path now. Skribs had no doubt whatsoever that she'd slaughter them all.

And he'd be there, beside her, or more likely behind her, fighting with the best of them.

But first, he was going to take out this piece of trash.

He hauled on the wrist of the hawk-faced man, jerked it upward and pinned him. Skribs leaned to the man's ear, and smiled. "No one touches the queen," he whispered, a salty breeze full of the promise of ice.

The little vial slipped from his pocket, and it was a matter of nothing to palm it under the man's nose, to watch as the man's eyes went wide with shocked recognition—to release him and watch as, horrified, the man went stumbling away, pushing courtiers aside in a most unseemly fashion.

So they were going to war against the North, were there?

Well. There went one fewer Northerner to threaten the queen.

Skribs tucked the recapped vial back into his pocket, and slowly drifted from the hall.

Lorelei would handle the fall out of her declaration of war just fine, and in about five minutes—or less, depending on how good the hawk-faced man's metabolism was—Skribs would have a corpse to vanish.

It might have been a touch blasé to whistle as he left the receiving hall—but Skribs was just a lanky, good-natured boy, and some impropriety was to be expected after all.

# THE MAKING OF *SOME IMPROPRIETY EXPECTED*

In 2020, I had the privilege of teaching a class of students who soon became some of my favourite people in the whole world. In the September of that year, I took a break from working on longer fiction to practise flash fiction some more, in particular a new technique for plotting that I'd just learned.

I was writing stories quite quickly, one every couple of days, and it seemed like Hard Work to keep thinking of character names I was happy with.

So I asked my class full of favourite people if they would mind if I borrowed their names. Nothing except the name and maybe the physical appearance of the character would reflect the original person, but they were welcome to read the finished story if they liked.

To my delight, they were all very happy to donate their names, and so began what turned into a two-year project as I dutifully wrote them all into stories.

This story, *Some Impropriety Expected*, is a scene from a future novel. Lorelei is the main character, although Skribs will have a point of view as well. It will follow Lorelei, newly crowned queen, as she attempts to demonstrate that it is possible to solve the problems of the kingdom without resorting to violence.

Whether or not she will be successful—whether or not it's even *possible* for such an endeavour to be successful? We'll all just have to read the book to find out.

For me, that's entirely the purpose of the exercise: to test the boundaries and constraints of the idea, and to explore its plausibility. *Is such a thing possible?*

I look forward to investigating.

# Read more by Amy Laurens!

# HOW NOT TO ACQUIRE A CASTLE

## *CHAPTER ONE*

ON A HARD PLASTIC CHAIR IN THE FRONT row of the Great Hall in the world's fifth-best evil overlording academy, with its red-wooden parquetry floor that spoke of wealth and the beige, square panels of sound-boards speaking of conservatism on the walls, Mercury sat, pointedly not sweating.

Partly, this was because the Academy Administrators had deigned to turn on the air-conditioning earlier in the day, in recognition of the fact that the hall would be packed out with approximately six hundred bodies, all here to celebrate the graduation of about a third of that crowd.

But mostly, Mercury was pointedly not sweating because she made it a point never to sweat, sweat being an indication that she was working hard, and hard work being antithetical to her way of life.

However. If she *had* been sweating right now, it would not have been due to the uncomfortable warmth of six hundred packed bodies that even the air-conditioning system couldn't completely shift, or, in fact, from overexertion. Instead, it would have been caused by an even more unfamiliar concept in Mercury's emotional vocabulary: nervousness.

Mercury did not *get* nervous. Mercury got things *done*.

So the fact that she was sitting here, in the front row of the Great Hall, about to graduate from Evil Overlording Academy (with distinction), and was feeling *nervous*... She crumpled the black paper program in her pale fists. It made her furious, that's what it did.

Abjectly furious, that snooty-tooty Deviran with his stupid morals and his stupid I-don't-want-to-be-here and his stupid Overlords-are-empty-figureheads and his stupid face sitting ten people over, looking implacable with his deep brown skin and barely-there, precision-groomed beard, as though he knew it gave him a stupid air of alluringly stupid mystery…

Mercury scowled and searched for the train of thought that had been derailed, yet again, by Deviran's stupidity.

Ah. Yes. She was angry because she was nervous because she wasn't absolutely entirely one hundred and fifty percent sure that she'd beaten Deviran in their final exams, and 1) being anything less than a hundred and fifty percent certain of anything made her cranky, and 2) being beaten by Deviran for dux of the year would be utterly unbearable. She flicked away a piece of fluff that had become snagged under her immaculately magenta-painted nails and smoothed out the black paper program.

In the front corner of the hall, the starkly-attired string quartet with their traditional black instruments began playing the March of the Oncoming Doom. The screechy scrapes of hundreds of chairs on the hall's wooden floor sounded as the crowd climbed to its collective feet.

Mercury sat with her arms firmly folded for a few moments longer, until her best friend Sparky kicked her in the ankle.

"Get up, idiot," Sparky hissed, hints of real flame flickering through her flame-coloured pixie cut.

"No," Mercury said, flouncing to her feet and tossing her own glossy brown hair back over her shoulders. Four years she'd been playing by the Academy's rules in order to get what she wanted, and she'd had just about enough. Other people's rules should only be applied to plebs too stupid to invent their own.

Sparky rolled her eyes somewhere over Mercury's head before focusing on the stage, where the ceremonial party had begun entering.

Mercury clenched her jaw and narrowed her own eyes as the teachers of the Evil Overlording Academy filed onto the stage, dressed in their formal finery. Each teacher had their own distinctive look that matched their personality and their Overlording style, from severe charcoal suits to jet-black leathers, pastel ball-gowns and gem-toned lingerie and eye-blinding spandex, and even on one tiny old woman at the back, worn jeans and a grey flannel shirt. She was the one to watch out for, of course; Mercury could respect an Overlord who was confident enough in their abilities that they didn't need to telegraph them. It wasn't a look *she* would consider, of course, but still. She could respect it.

The band's march finished and, after a moderately awkward pause, the crowd sat. The Principal, pale skin and dark hair matching his suspiciously vampiric red-and-black suit, took the podium, and Mercury narrowed her eyes. He was doing a superb job of hiding his emotions—he was a premier Evil Overlord, after all—but she was Mercury, and unlike anyone else, she had the benefit of being able to rummage through people's consciousnesses. She was better at adding things *into* people's minds than taking information out, but he was telegraphing fear loudly enough that she could sense it without trying overly much.

Mercury pursed her lips.

Hmm.

The Principal cleared his throat at the blackened-wood podium, and the fear made it into his usually-unreadable eyes. "Before we begin," he said, and Mercury's stomach did a peculiar kind of flip-flop. "I have a pressing announcement to make regarding the safety of our students and their families."

He cleared his throat again and took out a sheet of paper from his pocket, unfolding it carefully and smoothing out the creases before beginning again. "The Council"—quiet booing echoed around the hall, and Mercury tsked impatiently—"have asked me to recommend that students from Tumul Tuos seriously consider postponing their return to town for a few days. The city is dealing with a *situation* at present which may present a danger to our students' health and safety."

Mercury's hands fisted at her sides and she forced herself to remain seated. What was wrong with her city? What had the Council mucked up now? A risk to the students' safety? There had to be more he wasn't telling them. Gently, Mercury tugged on his consciousness, implanting the suggestion that it might be better to share the news than to keep it secret. After all, how could they fight an enemy they didn't know?

"There are, ah..." He trailed off, glancing side to side as though wondering why his mouth had decided to continue.

Mercury didn't snicker, but she did press her lips together in satisfaction.

The Principal took a deep, steadying breath and seemed to change tack. "There has been one death already. The family have already been notified, so it is with much regret that I must inform you that Woovermyer will no longer be with us at the Evil Overlording Academy."

Murmurs broke out around the room, not all of them sad—to be expected in a school devoted to raising the next generation of dictators (ish) and despots (of sorts).

Mercury, however, crushed her program in her left hand, fist so tight her nails bit her palm.

"You okay?" Sparky murmured.

Mercury gave a single, tense shake of her head and stared at the podium. Dead. Livie Woovermyer was dead in *her city*. And the Council hadn't done anything to stop it. Couldn't do anything to stop it, probably, given they'd warned the students to stay away. Livie hadn't been the strongest candidate in the year level, but she was no lightweight, either. It would take a lot of power to kill a Seven.

Enough was enough. A good thing Mercury was about to graduate at the top of the class, giving her the right to knock the lowest ranking current Overlord off their perch. Tumul Tuos would be hers in a matter of hours. And then there'd be no more of these wasteful deaths. Her city would be safe at last.

Madame Pompadour was up the front now, elbow gloves the same glimmery silver colour as her elaborate, piled-curls wig, eyelids gleaming with matching silver eye shadow, and abruptly Mercury realised Madame was there to make the announcement that would change her life forever. She leaned forward in her seat, ready to stand when her name was called.

"And now the announcement you've all been dying for," the Political Alliances teacher trilled, the frills on her evening gown fluttering as she moved. "The dux of this year's cohort!"

Sweat slicked Mercury's palms. Irritated, she reached over and wiped them on Sparky's thigh.

Sparky pushed Mercury's hands back into her own personal space bubble and Mercury, nervous to the edge of distraction, let her.

"Will you please join me in welcoming to the stage, our wonderful dux for this year, Deviran Goodsmith!"

Mercury froze halfway to standing. "Did she just say Deviran?" she whispered furiously to Sparky.

Sparky hauled her forcibly back down into her seat. "Yes," she hissed back. "Sit down, you're making a fool of yourself."

Mercury's spine snapped upright as she sat, and she arranged the folds of her long black skirt demurely. "No I'm not." She closed her eyes. "Deviran's going up to the stage, isn't he?" Even at a whisper, the misery in her voice was clear, but this time, she didn't care.

Sparky reached over and squeezed her hand.

Mercury squeezed back, lacing her fingers through Sparky's, and held tight as all her plans and dreams vanished in front of her.

A stone had landed in her chest. That must be it. Some strange sort of magic that made her chest contract and sink, and made the world distort for just a moment, long enough to trick her into thinking Deviran had beaten her so that someone could jump in front of her and yell SURPRISE!

Any moment now.

Any moment.

She refused to open her eyes and watch Deviran parading across the stupid stage like some stupid stupid-person, receiving his stupid medal and stupid symbolic crest pin.

It was that last exam question.

She'd known Deviran would pull out his ridiculous 'Evil Overlords are merely figureheads, the Business Guild is where the power really lies' rant that everyone had heard a million times back when he was younger and angrier, and she'd tried to counter it, she really had.

She'd argued for the importance of the Overlording position, for the power of having a symbolic figure to unite the population in their hatred, for having a person able to make all the difficult, necessary decisions the Council was too weak and spineless to make... But it hadn't been enough. Everything she'd worked for, everything she'd set out to prove—and it wasn't enough.

There were words, there were names, and then forever later, once she'd died twice already, Sparky elbowed her in the ribs. "Come on," Sparky muttered. "We're up next."

And sure enough, there was a shuffling of presenters as the last of the Powers Behind The Thone graduates departed the stage, and the next speaker announced in threatening, funereal tones, "The Over-lording cohort."

Mercury blinked furiously and followed Sparky to the end of the line at the right side of the stage. The other candidates proceeded one at a time across the stage, two girls and then stupid Deviran, and then a handful more and then Sparky, and then the speaker was calling her name.

Hands fisted, Mercury tossed her head high, climbed the four steps, and marched across the stage. She wouldn't look at them, the stupid faculty who'd denied her the city she rightfully deserved, and she wouldn't look the other way either, at the classmates and crowd undoubtedly sniggering at her failure.

She shook hands with the presenter, and while he pinned the tiny crossed-swords badge on her collar, her eyes betrayed her and slid towards the audience. Her stomach flipped as she saw the crowd of parents and friends behind the rows of students, all the way to the back of the hall, twenty rows at least, illuminated by the late afternoon light streaming in through the ceiling-high windows to the right. Everyone had someone here to watch them graduate. Everyone except Weird Al—and her.

The presenter finished with her pin, muttered something to her, and offered his hand again. Mercury coldly ignored it and strode from the stage. It didn't matter. None of it mattered. Tumul Tuos was her city anyway, and no one could change that. She'd think of something. She'd take a day or two out, make some plans...

And she could always hope that Deviran would choose some other Overlording territory. He'd be stupid to, but then again, he was stupid, so. Mercury could hope.

All at once, mid-way down the steps off the stage, Mercury came to rigid attention, scanning the room. Somewhere out there in the crowd, an exchange of power had just taken place, and it felt... unusual.

But the final few students were backing up behind her and muttering, so Mercury headed back toward her seat, craning her head all the while and searching for some sign of whatever it was that had just discharged a dizzyingly quiet amount of power into the room.

She sat, and Sparky leaned over. "Okay?"

"Mm," said Mercury. "Did you feel…" She accidentally caught the eye of the student behind her and twisted back to face the front.

"Feel what?"

Mercury turned it over in her mind. It had felt like a large shot of power discharged very quietly—but perhaps it hadn't been. Perhaps it had only been a small discharge after all, something most people wouldn't have noticed.

But still, something about it had tugged on her. It very nearly felt like something she'd felt before, only she *knew* she'd never sensed that kind of discharge before.

She shook her head. "Never mind. Don't worry."

Sparky sighed and straightened. "It's fine, Mercury," she said, drily exasperated. "I know you didn't win, but I promise, you'll live through it."

Mercury waved a hand for silence.

The power had just discharged again, and it had come from somewhere in the back corner, far away from the windows and light.

Impatiently, Mercury waited for the formalities to conclude. The crowd stood while the quartet played the exit march, and the stage party left, Mercury tapping her foot all the while.

The moment the last notes of the march died away, Mercury turned and headed to the back corner, weaving in and out of the students and parents who had seemed to explode slowly but inexorably out from the neat rows of seating, ignoring Sparky's calls behind her. Power, something that tugged in a way that was strange and familiar, all at once. She pushed her way through a family posing for pictures—and halted.

In the shadows of the back corner, Deviran stood with his family, with his stupid, smug little smile, looking as tall and dark and stupidly alluring as ever. Prat.

His mother, short but sleek, and his father—tall, and utterly terrifying in a way not at all diminished by his gleaming smile—gushed over him, patting his back and hugging him tight. Within moments the Principal was there, glibly shaking hands and congratulating them on the success of their son. Something flickered across his consciousness, and also Deviran's father's—some moment of recognition in response to what they were saying.

But Mercury brushed it aside just as the mother brushed melodramatic tears from her cheeks and handed Deviran a silver-wrapped package about as long as her hand but half the width.

That. That was the source of the strange, magical feeling. Mercury watched hawk-eyed as Deviran un-wrapped the gift. A glimpse of gold set her pulse racing—What was it? What did it do? Could she steal it?—and then the paper fell away to the floor, and Deviran stood staring wordlessly at the object in his hands, and Mercury did too.

Wide-eyed, Deviran raised his gaze to his parents, and even from where she stood Mercury could hear the reverence in his voice as he thanked them.

But Mercury had eyes only for the object. No wonder she'd felt it discharge, and no wonder it had felt both strange and familiar. In Deviran's hands lay a glorious, sunshine-gold key, large and strong—and with a handle in the shape of a stylised fish, long, flowing fins curving to make the grip.

A Key. They'd given him a Key. And not just any Key, but *the* Key, *her* Key, the Artefact of Power belonging to *her* city.

A wordless noise of wanting rose in Mercury's throat. Who cared about being dux? She needed that Key.

Keep reading! Head to<br>
www.amylaurens.com/books/<br>
kaditeos/castle<br>
to buy your copy now!

# ABOUT THE AUTHOR

AMY LAURENS is an Australian author of fantasy fiction for all ages. She does not generally recommend assassination as a way of solving your problems. Generally.

Amy's novella *Bones Of The Sea* won the 2021 Aurealis Award for Best Fantasy Novella. She has also written the award-winning portal-fantasy *Sanctuary* series about Edge, a 13-year-old girl forced to move to a small country town because of witness protection (the first book is *Where Shadows Rise*), the humorous fantasy *Kaditeos* series, following newly graduated Evil Overlord Mercury as she attempts to acquire a castle, the young adult series *Storm Foxes*, about love and magic and family in small town Australia, and a whole host of non-fiction.

# INKLETS

Collect them all! Released on the 1st and 15th of each month.

INKLET #075
Shadows
NEVER LIE
AMY LAURENS

INKLET #080
Here She Lies
LIANA BROOKS

INKLET #081
Perfect
Destruction
An Age Of Unicorns Story
AMY LAURENS

INKLET #082
What Blood
Can Do
AMY LAURENS

INKLET #083
Dancer, Dreamer
Seer
LIANA BROOKS

INKLET #084
As Time
Whirls Slowly
Past
AMY LAURENS

INKLET #085
Far More
Satisfying
Than Hell
AMY LAURENS

INKLET #086
Just
Another Day
In Hell
LIANA BROOKS

INKLET #087
Moon AND
Morning
AMY LAURENS

INKLET #089
Some
Impropriety
Expected
AMY LAURENS

INKLET #089
NEON SNOW
LIANA BROOKS

INKLET #090
Reincarnation
LIANA BROOKS

INKLET #091
More Than
Mushrooms
AMY LAURENS

DOUBLE ISSUE
INKLET #092
How To Make A Star
& The World Ended
LIANA BROOKS

INKLET #093
CAUGHT
IN THE ACT
AMY LAURENS

INKLET #094
ANUBIS
Has Sent You
Six Souls
LIANA BROOKS

INKLET #095
PRAYER TO A
GODDESS
LIANA BROOKS

INKLET #096
Love In The
Time Of Corona
AMY LAURENS

www.ingramcontent.com/pod-product-compliance
Lightning Source LLC
Chambersburg PA
CBHW030813190726
48285CB00003B/1154